Stink

Megan McDonald

illustrated by

K and the **Shark** **Sleepover**

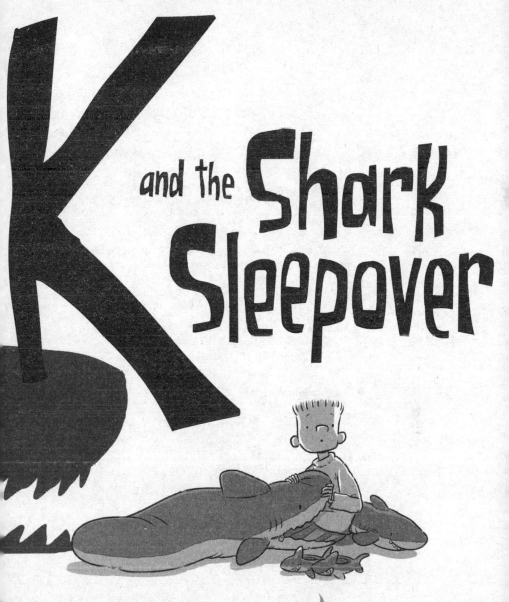

Peter H. Reynolds

CANDLEWICK PRESS

Text copyright © 2014 by Megan McDonald
Illustrations copyright © 2014 by Peter H. Reynolds
Interior illustrations created by Matt Smith

First paperback edition 2015

Library of Congress Catalog Card Number 2013943081
ISBN 978-0-7636-6474-9 (hardcover)
ISBN 978-0-7636-7678-0 (paperback)

19 20 21 22 23 MVP 15 14 13 12 11

Printed in York, PA, U.S.A.

This book was typeset in Stone Informal and hand-lettered by the illustrator. The illustrations were created digitally.

Candlewick Press
99 Dover Street
Somerville, Massachusetts 02144

visit us at www.candlewick.com

for Dee
M. M.

To all the fish in all the ponds, lakes,
streams, and oceans around the world
and to all the kids reading this book
who will work to save them
P. H. R.

CONTENTS

Sleepy.

Sleepier.

Sleepiest. . . . NOT!

Stink had to wait. Wait and wait and wait some more for Mom and Dad to come home from their fancy dance. Chloe, the babysitter, was pop-pop-popping popcorn in the kitchen.

"Trying to stay awake is worse than holding your breath underwater," Stink told Judy. He yawned.

"Why don't you just go to bed?" Judy asked.

"Because Mom and Dad went to a thingy."

"Uh-huh. A fund-raiser thingy."

"And it raises money for your heart."

"So?"

"So they get to bid on prizes and they might win stuff."

"And?"

"And if they win the best prize, I get a trip to Montpelier." Stink yawned.

"The capital of Vermont?"

"No, not Vermont. James Madison's house. Right here in Virginia."

"I should have known," said Judy.

"You get to cook on a fire and dig for old stuff." Stink yawned some more. "And make a brick."

"Vermont would be cooler," said Judy. "Vermont has teddy bears and maple syrup and Vermontasaurus."

Stink did not hear a word Judy said about Vermont. He had fallen asleep right smack-dab in the middle of the family-room floor, curled up next to Charlie (creepy puppet), Astro (guinea pig), Toady (toad), and Mouse (cat). And Hoodoo, Voodoo, Gilgamesh, and Fred (yarn zombies).

Chloe came back with the popcorn. "Aww. He looks so sweet when he's asleep."

"A sleeping Stink is a good thing," said Judy.

* * *

"We're home!" called Mom and Dad. "Anybody up?"

Stink popped up as if he'd never been asleep. "Did we win?"

Mom rubbed her feet. Dad took off his tie. Mom hung up her purse. Dad and Mom said good-bye to Chloe. Chloe waved good-bye to Judy and Stink.

Stink looked from Mom to Dad. "So, did we win? Did we, did we, did we?"

"We won," said Dad. "I won an antique doorstop."

Stink's face fell.

"Dad's kidding," said Mom. "*I* won. An autographed cookbook."

"What?" said Stink. "The only thing worse than a doorstop is a cookbook!"

"Good-bye, Vermont," said Judy. "Hello, meatloaf."

"So no trip to James Madison's house?" asked Stink.

"We *did* win a trip," said Dad.

"But not to James Madison's house," said Mom.

Stink's heart sank. "To where, then?"

"The aquarium!" said Mom in a much too chipper voice.

Stink's shoulders sank. "The aquarium? The aquarium is not Montpelier. The aquarium is not James Madison's house."

"Although you could say James Madison *is* sleeping with the fishes," Dad joked.

"But *this* trip," said Mom, "is a *sleepover*."

"Uh-oh," Judy said under her breath.

"You get to see the aquarium *after* it closes," said Dad. "And spend the night."

"Double uh-oh," Judy mumbled.

"You *sleep* there the whole night?" Stink asked. "Till the next morning?"

"Stink's afraid of sleepovers," said Judy.

"Am not!" said Stink.

"What about the time you tried to sleep over at Webster's, and his glow-in-the-dark *Star Wars* poster freaked you out so bad, you came home at eight o'clock?"

"So? Vader was staring a hole right through me."

"And the sleepover at Grandma Lou's? The time you heard a ghost?"

"There really *was* a chipmunk in her attic!" said Stink. "You were scared, too."

"Kids," Dad warned.

"Besides," said Stink. "I was only seven then."

"You're still seven."

"Seven and *three quarters*." Stink turned to Mom and Dad. "Will there be sharks?" Stink asked eagerly.

"There will be sharks," said Dad.

Stink took in a breath. "Yippee!" he yelled. "A shark sleepover!"

"No fair," said Judy. "How come I never got to go on a big-deal, fancy sleepover?"

"We'll tag along, too," Dad told Judy. "It's for the whole family."

"Double yippee!" said Judy.

"And Stink can invite a friend," said
Mom.

Stink ran upstairs. He came back
with his arms full of stuff. Shark stuff.

"What is all this junk?" Judy asked.

"It's for the big sleepover. There's
my shark sleeping bag and Leroy my
stuffed tiger shark that I use for a pillow sometimes and my *Big Mouth Book
of Sharks.*"

"Is that all?" Judy teased.

"Oh. Yeah. I can't forget to wear my
shark-tooth necklace."

"The sleepover's not till Friday," said
Dad.

"So?" Stink ran upstairs again and came back wearing slippers on his hands. "Check it out. Shark slippers."

Just then, the phone rang. Judy answered it. After a little while she said, "Stink, it's for you."

"For me? Who is it?"

"It's Sophie the Shark-Sleepover Stealer," Judy whispered.

"Huh?" Stink grabbed the phone. "Hello?"

"Guess what?" said Sophie of the Elves. "I just found out I won a trip to the aquarium. A sleepover!"

"But I just won a trip to the aquarium," said Stink.

"I know! My mom said there were two prizes. We *both* won! And guess who I'm inviting? Webster!"

"I was going to invite Webster, too," said Stink.

"Yay! So all three of us get to go on the sleepover together!"

"Sweet," said Stink.

Stink slipped the shark slippers on his feet this time. He rubbed his shark-tooth necklace. "Shark Sleepover, here we come!"

TANKS A LOT!

The Georgia Aquarium in Atlanta is the world's largest aquarium. The shark tank alone holds 6.3 million gallons of water. Whoa!

The Shanghai Ocean Aquarium has the longest underwater viewing tunnel in the world at 492 feet. That's as long as five basketball courts.

The aquarium at uShaka Marine World in South Africa is built from an old cargo ship to imitate a shipwreck.

Shark attack — at the mall! When a 33-ton tank in a Chinese shopping center burst, lemon sharks spilled out into the crowd!

Finally, it was Friday. Shark Sleepover night!

When the Moodys got to the aquarium, Stink spotted Webster right away. He was waiting outside with Sophie of the Elves, Sophie's mom, and her little sister. "Sophie! Webster!" yelled Stink. Sophie waved, holding her *Big Head Book of Elves, Faeries, Mermaids, Pixies, and Other Wee Folk* in one hand and her little sister, Mimi's, hand in the other. The Moodys joined them in line.

Stink hauled his shark sleeping bag under one arm and slung his back-pack, stuffed to the gills with shark stuff, over his shoulder.

"What did you bring, Webster?" Stink asked.

"I brought Go Fish and Critter Concentration in case we get bored. A

baloney sandwich and ketchup packets in case I get hungry. And one of my Hug Uglies in case I get scared."

"Wow. You thought of everything."

"I also brought my blue-shark Tooth-Fairy pillow," said Webster. He grinned, wiggling his loose tooth for his friends to see. "For my looth tooth."

"Your looth tooth?" Stink and Sophie cracked up.

"It's hard to say *looth tooth* when you have a looth tooth!" The letter *S* came out funny. They cracked up again. "This way I'm ready for the Tooth Fairy, in case my you-know-what falls out tonight at the you-know-where."

"Whoa. Did you know sharks lose around thirty-five thousand teeth in their lifetime?" Stink asked.

"That's a lot of Tooth Fairy," said Webster.

"If we were sharks, we'd be rich!" said Stink.

Sophie's little sister poked Stink. "You're Stinky," said Mimi.

"I'm Stink," said Stink. "Not Stinky."

"Stinky, Stinky, Stinky," said Mimi, dancing around in circles in her tutu.

"Are you ready for the Shark Sleepover?" asked Webster.

"Don't say *shark* around You-Know-Who," said Sophie, nodding at Mimi.

"Well, don't say *sleepover* around You-Know-Stink," said Judy. Stink gave Judy a stop-saying-I'm-afraid-of-sleepovers-in-front-of-my-friends look.

Tons of people crowded outside the side entrance. There were kids and families, Cub Scouts, a Brownie troop, and a soccer team. Webster nudged Stink and nodded to a group of noisy girls holding sleeping bags.

"Oh, no," said Stink, "It's Riley Rottenberger. Quick, make yourselves invisible."

But it was too late. Riley came over. "Hey! Who knew you guys were going to be here?"

"We knew," said Stink. "But what are *you* doing here?"

"I'm here with my FINS group." She waved a bunch of girls over. "This is

Hannah, Anna, Emma, Olivia, and Maisy."

"Fins?" asked Sophie.

"Friends in Nature Study," said Riley.

"But you hate nature," said Stink. Emma and Maisy looked shocked.

"Do not," said Riley. "Well, maybe *outside* nature. But this is *inside* nature."

"This is our *third* FINS sleepover," said one of the FINS.

"Our last one was a Flower Power sleepover at the Flower Palace," said Riley.

"Uh-huh," said Stink, nodding. He craned his neck, trying to see through the glass doors into the aquarium.

"We saw plants that ate bugs."

"Uh-huh." Stink was hardly listening.

"And made duct-tape flowers."

"Uh-huh."

"And we ate worms in dirt."

"Huh?" said Stink.

"Gotcha!" said Riley. "It was really

gummy worms in chocolate pudding."
Riley turned to her friends.

"Stink is my study buddy from school," Riley told the FINS. "Right, Stink?"

Stink gulped. "I am?"

"He likes Pluto and stuff," Riley told them. "And we like to bug each other."

"We?" asked Stink. "*You* bug *me*."

"Yuck, yuck, yuck. See? Isn't he funny?" Riley cackled. "Hey, guess what, Stink! I got a good game for you. It's called Would You Rather. Would you rather . . . freeze your butt off on Pluto at minus three hundred degrees *or* get your insides sucked out by a giant sea anemone?"

Riley's friends giggled. Webster shivered. Sophie made a sourball face.

"Riley Rottenberger," said Stink. "With friends like you, who needs anemones?"

* * *

As soon as the aquarium doors opened, all the sleepover groups rushed inside. Tour guides in blue aquarium shirts passed out name tags and packets of information.

"Stink," said Dad, "we'll go with Sophie's family to stake out a good spot for our sleeping bags. Judy, do you want to stay with Stink and his friends?"

"Second graders? No way," said Judy, shaking her head.

"Have fun, Stink," said Mom. "We'll catch up with you later."

Stink, his friends, and the other groups sat on the floor in the center of the rotunda, just outside the Turtletorium. A milky-green sea turtle with a lost flipper munched on a head of lettuce.

"My name is—well, you can call me Miss D.," said their tour guide. "Tonight, we'll explore a touch pool

together and go on a sea-creature scavenger hunt. There will also be an indoor campfire with snacks later. I'll be your guide for the evening. If you have questions, just ask me or anybody with a blue shirt on."

"Will there be sharks?" asked Stink.

"There will be sharks," said Miss D.

"Do we really have to go to sleep?" asked Riley.

"Yes, you really have to go to sleep. But not till we've had a fun evening."

"What does the *D* stand for?" asked Sophie.

"Excuse me?"

"Your name. Miss D. Does the *D* stand for *Dolphin?*"

"The *D* is not for *Dolphin.*"

"Is it for *Dungeon?* How about *Dragon?*" asked Webster.

"Sorry," said Miss D. "Now, if you'll all follow me, we'll start with—"

"Sharks?" asked Stink, crossing his fingers. "Please say sharks."

"Touch pools," said Miss D. "Follow me to the Starfish Enterprise."

They left the sea turtles and went past the gift shop. Stink could hear dolphins splashing in the next room as they came to two large open tanks.

Groups of kids peered into the tide pool. Sea stars clung to rocks. Anemones waved tentacles. Crabs skittered, and snails slithered.

"Baby octoputh!" Webster shouted. But the octopus was just a rock with spots. "False alarm," he said.

"See all those shells?" said Sophie. "Are those hermit crabs?"

"Sure are," said Miss D., picking one up. Tiny red legs, one big purple claw, and two antennas poked out of the shell.

"Hermit crabs are my favorite," said Sophie. Just then, Mimi ran up to Sophie.

"Crabby, crabby, crabby," she said, pointing.

"These guys are ocean hermit crabs," Miss D. told everybody.

"Do they change shells?" asked Sophie.

"They sure do. When they get too big

for their shells, they find a bigger home to move into, like an empty snail shell. But sometimes a hermit crab can't find a shell, and it moves into something like an old can or bottle."

"I had a hermit crab." Riley talked a mile a minute. "One time, my dad dropped his pen cap in the tank and the hermit crab used it for his home."

"Is that true?" asked Stink. Riley Rottenberger told tall tales.

"Of course it's true, Stink Moody."

Stink looked at Riley. "A noisy noise annoys an oyster," said Stink.

Webster and Sophie cracked up. "Ha, ha," said Riley. "But you're not an oyster. So how can I annoy you?"

"Okay, then, a noisy noise annoys a *boy*-ster."

Listen up, people," said Miss *D*-is-not-for-*Dungeon*-or-*Dragon*. She passed out maps and scavenger-hunt sheets. "Who's ready to be a detective?"

"*D* is for *Detective!*" said Sophie. "Miss Detective?"

"Afraid not," said Miss D. "But *S* is for *scavenger hunt.*"

Everybody got into teams.

"Our team is gonna beat you, Stink Moody," said Riley Rottenberger. "We're the Rotten Eggs—for *Rotten*berger. Get it?"

"I get it. The last one to finish will be a Rotten Egg," said Stink. He cracked himself up. Riley and the Rotten Eggs headed off.

"Let's be Team Sharkfinder," Stink said. "We can be the ones to find Sharkzilla on the scavenger hunt."

Sophie shivered. Webster wiggled his loose tooth. "Who's Tharkzilla?"

"Don't you guys watch Shark Week?" Stink asked. "Sharkzilla is a megalodon.

He's like the world's biggest shark that lived around ten million years ago."

"What did he look like?" asked Webster.

"He was more than fifty feet long and he weighed as much as a house. And he had two hundred and fifty teeth. They say he would be able to bite through a car."

"Yikes," said Sophie. "But he's not real, right?"

"He was. He was like a dinosaur shark," said Stink. "They made a model of him for Shark Week. Like a shark robot with giant chompers made of steel. He bit through a mini fridge, a Jet Ski, and a red couch in one bite."

Webster felt for his loose tooth to make sure it was still there. "Is he here?"

"I wish! But I read they have one of his fins here. It's seven feet tall and you can get your picture taken with it."

"This is megalo-not-boring," said Sophie. "But everybody else already started the scavenger hunt."

"First we have to find something that looks like a horse," said Stink.

They followed the map, turning it this way and that until they came to Sea Horse Alley—a dark hallway lined with glass aquariums. There were spiny sea horses and pygmy sea horses. There were sea horses with fat tummies and sea horses that looked like they had the measles.

"What took you guys so long?" Riley and the Rotten Eggs called.

"Looks like Team Rotten beat us here," said Webster.

"What's next?" asked Sophie.

"Next we find something that looks like a bat," said Stink.

They wandered past the Sponge Zone and the Octopus's Garden. They gazed up at wolf eels and schools of sardines and señoritas swimming through the swaying fronds of the kelp forest.

At last, they came to Manta Ray Magic.

In no time, they spotted the bat ray. "Na-na-na-na-na-na-na-na—Bat Ray!" sang Stink and Webster.

"Bat rays lose tons of teeth from crushing shells to eat stuff," said Stink.

"Just like me!" said Webster.

Riley walked past the Sharkfinders on her way out of Manta Ray Magic. "We are the Rotten Eggs," she said to them, trying to sound like a bad guy from a Batman movie. "Learn it well, Stink Moody. It is the sound of your doom."

Stink turned to his friends. "Hurry up, guys. Now we have to find some-thing that looks like a brain."

"Half the stuff in the aquarium looks like a brain," said Webster.

Seals barked in the background as Team Sharkfinder entered Nemo's Reef. Wall-to-wall fish tanks held colorful clown fish playing hide-and-seek among sea anemones and neon-bright coral. One looked just like a floating brain!

They all took a moment to gaze in amazement at the eerie, greenish, glow-in-the-dark brain coral.

But Riley and her Rotten Eggs had beaten them to it again.

"What did one brain say to the other brain?" asked Riley.

Stink shrugged. "I'm going to outsmart you, Team Sharkfinder."

Clue by clue, the Sharkfinders found a porcupine fish, a fairy penguin, and an electric eel.

But the Rotten Eggs were one step ahead of them all the way.

Last of all, they had to find something with two hundred fifty teeth that could bite through a car.

Sophie looked at Stink. Stink looked at Webster. Their eyes grew wide. "Sharkzilla!" they yelled, jumping up and down.

Suddenly, Judy came rushing up to Stink, all out of breath. "There you are! I was . . . Mom and Dad and I . . . you gotta go . . . Hall of Wonders, Stink."

"Not now. We just have one more thing to find in the scavenger hunt. And we have to beat the Rotten Eggs."

"Trust me, Stinker. You *don't* want to miss this."

"Okay, okay, but make it fast."

Stink and his friends hurried after Judy, who led them to the Hall of Wonders. There, just inside the entrance, was a shiny, silvery, seven-foot shark fin!

Is this . . . was this . . . could it be? "Sharkzilla's fin!" yelled Stink. He held both hands up to high-five Judy.

"You won! Good for you," said Miss D., popping out from behind Sharkzilla's fin. "You're the first ones to finish the scavenger hunt. And as a prize for finishing first, you win the Shark Fin Award." Miss D. handed them shark fin T-shirts that said I HAD A FIN TIME AT THE AQUARIUM.

Stink rubbed his hand along the giant fin. "Is this the real Sharkzilla's fin? From the model built for Shark Week?"

"One and the same," said Miss D.

"*D* is for *Dinosaur*?" asked Sophie, hopefully.

"Wrong again," said Miss D., shaking her head. "Keep guessing."

Just then, Riley Rottenberger and her team came rushing into the Hall of Wonders.

"Last one to find Sharkzilla is a Rotten Egg!" cried Stink.

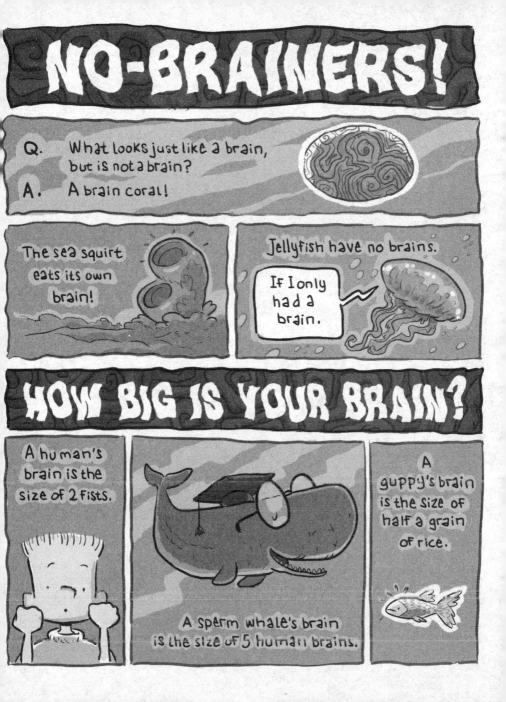

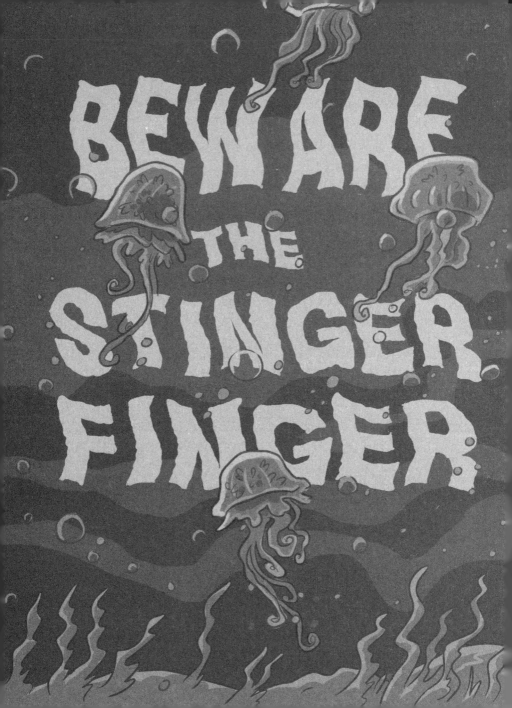

Is it time to go to sleep yet?" asked Webster.

"Not even close," said Sophie.

"Is it time for sharks?" Stink asked Miss D.

"It's time for . . . jellyfish." The sleepover kids followed Miss D. past the Wall of Fish to the Planet of the Jellies. Mimi ran up to Sophie, clutching a red-haired mermaid. Her face was streaked with tears. Sophie's mom pulled Sophie aside to talk to her.

In every tank, ooey-gooey, creepy-deepy blobs danced and glowed, zoomed and bloomed in the water. There were blue, green, and pink jellies. There were purple-striped jellies and white-spotted jellies. There were upside down jellies and rainbow-colored glow-in-the-dark jellies.

"I hope we get to sleep here," said Webster. "Sleeping with jellyfith would be cool."

"Everybody knows you don't sleep at a sleepover, right Sophie?" Stink looked around. "Sophie?"

"Here I am," said Sophie, coming up behind them.

"Hey, what's wrong with Mimi?" asked Stink.

"She got scared and won't go to sleep, so Mom has to take her home."

"Does that mean we have to go?" asked Webster.

"Nope. My mom talked to Stink's mom and we get to stay with the Moodys."

"Phew," said Stink.

"Phew," said Webster.

"Too bad about your little sister," said Eagle-Ears Riley. "She probably couldn't sleep because she was afraid of getting stung by the world's deadliest box jelly. Or whiplashed by a bat ray. Or eaten by a tiger shark."

Stink turned as white as a ghost shrimp. "Check out this jellyfish," he said, changing the subject. "It looks like a broken egg."

"That one over there looks like a plate," said Webster.

"Look at the one that's wearing a hula skirt," said Sophie.

"That was the egg-yolk jellyfish, the

dinner-plate jellyfish, and the hula-skirt jellyfish," said a man in a blue shirt.

"No lie?" asked Stink.

"No lie," said the man.

"Everybody," said Miss D., "this is Marco."

"Polo!" said Webster.

"Marco is our resident jellyfish wrangler," said Miss D.

"Cool-o," said Stink.

Marco laughed. "Welcome to Planet of the Jellies. Jellyfish are unusual because they don't have brains or bones or blood. Or teeth or fins.

"Over here, we have the giant lion's mane jelly. Its body can grow up to eight feet around and more than eight feet long. Add its tentacles, and it can be longer than a blue whale—the biggest mammal on Earth."

"Whoa," said Stink.

"It has a deadly sting. Sherlock Holmes even solved a mystery where the murder weapon was a sting from a lion's mane."

"Hey, Stink," Riley asked, "would you rather get stung by a Portuguese man-of-war or an Australian box jellyfish?"

"A Portuguese man-of-war sting is like getting struck by lightning," said Stink. "And an Australian box jellyfish has enough poison to kill sixty people. So neither."

"Here comes the blue blubber jelly,"

said Marco. All the kids watched the eerie blue blob pulse to its own rhythm.

"It looks like a bell," said Sophie.

"Sea turtles love to eat these," said Marco.

"Do they eat the stinging part?" asked Riley.

"They sure do," said Marco. "Guess what. People in China and Japan like to eat jellyfish, too."

"No way!" said Riley's friend Maisy.

"Yes way," said Marco. "I tried it once."

"Ooh. What do they taste like?" asked Stink.

"Think of a rubber-band salad," said Marco.

"Yuck!" said Maisy.

"Someday you just might eat a peanut-butter-and-jellyfish sandwich," said Marco.

"No way!" said Stink.

"This red guy here is the bloodybelly comb jelly. It lives in the ocean. If it swallows any prey that glows, the red helps to hide it from predators."

"Ooh. Gross. It looks like a kidney. Or a heart," said Webster.

"Are you ready for a smack?" Marco asked. Stink jumped back.

Marco chuckled. "I don't mean a slap. A *smack* of jellyfish. That's what you call a group of jellies. Here they come." A smack of jellies floated by like small spaceships.

"Don't they look lip-smacking good?" Marco asked.

"Eeew!" everybody groaned.

"Look, they're all swimming upside down," said Riley.

"Invasion of the Mushroom Planet!" said Stink.

"And that one has a blue belly button," said Sophie.

"That's his *jelly* button," said Stink.

"Good one," said Marco.

The dark room was hushed while people watched the creatures float, swim, and sail through the water.

"Before I go, I want to show y'all one last thing." Marco put a hand into the tank and dragged it through the water. Some of the jellies lit up and glowed in the dark. They floated and tumbled and turned and danced, putting on quite a light show.

"See? You didn't know you had tickets to the Moon Jelly Ballet, did you?"

"I read that jellyfish went to outer space," said Stink. "Is that true?"

"It's absolutely true. Thousands of moon jelly babies rode on the shuttle *Columbia* so scientists could study how they'd grow in outer space."

"Invasion of the jelly aliens!" said Stink. "The Jellians!"

"So, who would like to help me light up the jellies?" asked Marco.

"No way!" "Gross!" "Are you nuts?"

Marco looked at Webster.

"Not me," said Webster. "Even dead jellyfith sting."

Stink raised his hand. "I'll try."

Marco showed Stink where to put his hand in the tank. The jellies lit up

and glowed like a string of blue and white twinkle lights.

"Moon jellies make the best night-lights ever!" said Stink.

"Night-lights are for babies," Riley said. Stink gave her the stink eye. As he did, his hand brushed against a jelly. "Aagh! My finger!" Stink pulled his hand away super fast.

"Did you get stung?" asked Webster.

"No. Just cooties. Good thing only this finger touched it," said Stink, holding up the index finger on his right hand.

"Gross! Jellyfish cooties!" said Riley.

Stink waved the Jellyfish Finger in the air. "Stinger Finger!" he cried. All six of the FINS backed away.

"I thought I wanted to be a pro smeller for NASA," said Stink. "But now I want to be a jellyfish wrangler. I could change my name to Sting."

Marco reached out to shake Stink's hand. "Good to meet you, Sting."

When do we get to see sharks?" Stink asked.

"Follow me to Sharks Ahoy!" Miss D. called out.

"Cool!" said Stink. "Dun-dun, dun-dun," he sang as they walked around the rotunda, past penguins splashing in the Palace of Ice, and up a spooky, green-lit ramp.

They followed Miss D. into a glass tunnel that went right through the shark tank. Sleek, slippery sharks swam around them on all sides. Stink gazed in silent awe at the monsters of the deep, with their black beady eyes, pointy snouts, and razor-sharp teeth.

At last, Miss D. broke the silence. "Here we have a shiver of sand tiger sharks."

"They're all teeth," said Sophie, shivering. "That one needs braces!"

"Sand tiger sharks go through over three thousand teeth in their lifetime. They look mega-mean, like the great whites," said Miss D., "but they aren't really known to attack humans."

"Awethome," said Webster, fiddling with his loose tooth again.

"Just think," said Stink. "If we lost three thousand teeth, and we got a dollar from the tooth fairy for each one we lost, we'd have three thousand dollars!"

"Sharks have an amazing sense of smell," said Miss D.

"Me, too," said Stink.

"Yes, but could you smell one drop of blood in a million drops of water? That's about twenty-five gallons."

"No way," said Stink.

"And did you know sharks burp?" said Miss D.

"They do not," said Rotten Riley.

"I'm afraid so. These sharks come up to the surface, gulp in air, and hold it in their stomachs. This helps them float."

"*Burrrp!*" Riley burped on purpose.

"Do sharks have boogers, too?" asked Anna.

"Shark snot!" said Riley.

"So, who wants to touch a shark? Anybody?" asked Miss D.

The room fell super quiet. "Stink will," said Riley. Three of the FINS started urging Stink forward.

"*Snot* after that!" said Stink.

"You can touch it with your Jellyfish Finger," said Riley. "Since it already has cooties."

"I was only kidding," said Miss D.

"Phew," said Stink. "I thought you were serious."

"But if you *did* touch a shark, it wouldn't feel smooth. A shark's skin is sandpapery, like a cat's tongue."

"Miss D., have you ever touched a shark?" asked Sophie.

"I have."

"So is the *D* for *Dangerous*?"

"You're getting warmer," said Miss D., smiling.

Just then, a spotted shark swam by.

"This toothy guy right here," said Miss D., "is Mr. Spock. Can you guess what his favorite TV show is?"

"*Star Trek!*" said Webster.

"*Shark* Trek," said Miss D. Stink and his friends cracked up. Then they gave Mr. Spock a Vulcan hand salute.

"Sand tiger sharks feed at night, so who would like to go behind the scenes and watch a shark eating dinner?"

Several hands went up in the air.

Miss D. pointed to Stink and his friends. "Why don't you three come with me? The rest of you can head to the gift shop until it's your turn."

"I'm with them," said Riley Rottenberger, sliding in next to Stink.

"No, she's—"

"That's fine," said Miss D. "After me." Miss D. led them to a catwalk over the tanks. From up there they could see pipes and tanks and more pipes!

"That's our wave-making machine," said Miss D. over the roar of the water.

"The sharks swim in a tank that holds over six million gallons."

"Who knew Niagara Falls was up here," said Stink.

"Stink," said Riley. "Would you rather go over Niagara Falls without a raft *or* fall off Mount Rushmore without a parachute?"

"I'd rather watch a stuntman do those things in a movie," said Stink.

"Would you rather get bitten by a moray eel *or* chomped on by a tiger shark?"

Stink shifted from one foot to the other, thinking it over.

"What's the matter? Shark got your tongue?" Riley cracked herself up.

"I'd rather the moray eel bite the tiger shark," said Stink.

"Here's Ariel," said Miss D. "She's getting ready to feed Mr. Spock."

"What does she feed the sharks?" Sophie asked.

"Fish, mostly. They like bony fish. And squid. And skates."

Ariel took a silvery fish from a bucket and attached it to a long pole. She stuck the pole in the water and *SMACK!* The shark attacked the pole, chomping down with his huge jaws

and—presto—in the blink of an eye, the fish was gone. Mr. Spock gulped the whole thing in one big bite.

"Shark attack!" said Riley.

"That was mega scary," said Sophie.

"Mega creepy," said Riley. "But I wasn't scared."

"Mega awesome!" said Stink. "That was jawsome!"

★ ★ ★

Stink, Sophie, and Webster went to the gift shop before it closed. The shop had stuffed sharks and starfish. Mermaid dolls and robot crabs.

Stink and his friends zoomed around, looking at stuff.

"Stink," said Rotten Riley. "Would you rather be crushed by two tons of beach plastic *or* get sucked into the Great Pacific Garbage Vortex and never come out?"

"Great Pacific Garbage *Patch*. I'd build a giant raft out of all the plastic trash and sail my way out."

Riley ran off to check out the plush penguins with her fellow FINS.

"Psst. Stinkerbell. Over here."

Stink swiveled around and peered through a rack of puppets. Judy!

"Can I borrow some money, Stinker?"

"What for?"

"For a Siamese fighting fish. They build bubble nests out of spit."

"Sorry. I'm all out of money."

"But I thought you had ten dollars?"

"Not any more. I adopted a shark. I'm giving the money to the aquarium to help feed a tiger shark."

"Good thing," Judy said. "I don't think a tiger shark would fit in the bathtub." Stink cracked up.

"I can't decide what to get," said Webster. "A man-eating shark hat or a kit to build a model of *Plastiki* out of recycled stuff."

"*Plastiki!*" said Stink.

"What's *Plastiki*?" asked Judy.

"It's a real-live boat that a crew of people built out of plastic bottles," said Webster. "They sailed it across the ocean to Australia so people would stop and think about all the plastic that ends up in the ocean."

"Rare," said Judy. "Sophie, what are you getting?"

Sophie held up a hermit crab habitat. The small tank had a palm tree, a bridge, a sponge, and a water dish.

A tiny crab poked out of a coconut-shell hut. "I got a real pet hermit crab! Pinchers and all." She reached over and pinched Stink's arm.

"Youch!" said Stink. "The Stinger Finger is going to get you!"

"What's its name?" asked Judy.

"Mr. Crab Cakes," said Sophie.

"I had a hermit crab once," said

Judy. "His name was Harvey. He came to a bad end."

"Please don't tell that story," said Stink. "I mean it."

"Tell it!" said Webster and Sophie.

Stink stuck his fingers in his ears. *"Row, row, row your boat . . ."* he sang.

Judy pulled Stink's hands away from his ears.

"Stink, I promise I won't tell your friends about the time Harvey the Hermit Crab was in my pocket and he went through the washing machine—tsunami city!" Judy zipped her lips. "My lips are sealed."

PLASTIKI

What boat is made out of 12,500 recycled plastic bottles? *Plastiki!*

Plastiki sailed 8,000 miles from San Francisco, California, to Sydney, Australia.

Line Islands

Tuvalu

Plastiki was built to make people aware of the 73.9 million pounds of plastic trash floating in our oceans.

Plastiki was named after *Kon-Tiki*, a raft that sailed across the Pacific from South America in 1947 to prove that the journey could be made without much equipment.

Stink glanced at the clock. Uh-oh. It was getting closer and closer to the *sleep* part of the sleepover.

Miss D. turned out the lights in the rotunda. Glow-in-the-dark stars were hanging from the domed ceiling, making it look like a night sky.

"*D* is for *Dark*?" Sophie asked Miss D. "Miss Darkness?"

Miss D. shook her head no. Miss *D-is-not-for-Darkness* took out her laptop and projected some flames up on the wall. The flames flickered and popped and glowed.

"It looks like a real campfire!" said Webster.

Miss D. shook a spray can and gave the air a few tiny squirts.

"I smell nature," said Riley.

"I smell Christmas trees," said Sophie.

"I smell s'mores," said Webster.

"It's pine forest mist air freshener," said Miss D.

"It smells like a real campfire!" said Stink.

Everybody sat in a circle around a virtual campfire (battery-operated candles). They pretended to roast (real) marshmallows over the (pretend) fire.

Before long, Sophie started to slump. Webster's eyelids started to droop. "Guys!" said Stink. "You can't fall asleep yet. You have to stay awake for midnight snack at ten o'clock. Waffles!"

Stink tried to think of something

that would keep them awake. He saw
a door just off the ramp to Sharks Ahoy
that said KEEP OUT.

"What's behind that door?" Stink
asked Miss D.

"Don't you know?" Miss D. asked in
an almost-whisper.

"Tell us!" everybody said, perking
right up. "Tell us, tell us, tell us."

"This is the story about a creature
who lived right here in this very aquarium. See that dark, empty tank? That
was her home, once upon a time."

"Her who?" everybody asked.

"They called her Bloody Mary. She was a vampire squid."

"Oooh."

"Bloody Mary had dripping red tentacles, glowing red eyes, and she lurked at the very way bottom of the deepest, darkest ocean tank. She was a creature the color of blood."

"Is this true?" asked Riley.

"Vampire squids are strange monsters of the deep. What do you think Bloody Mary ate?"

"Fish?" asked Olivia.

"Shark meat?" asked Hannah.

"Hermit crabs?" asked Riley.

"Only if they were dead. Bloody Mary ate only dead and rotting things—eyes and legs and tails and poop, carcasses and corpses, and snot and other gunk that sank to the bottom of her tank."

"Is *that* true?" asked Riley.

"Cross my heart," said Miss D. "Vampire squids have two long filaments like arms, which they use to reach out and grab dead stuff floating in the sea. Then they slime it with mucus and eat it all in one gulp."

"Stink," said Riley. "Would you rather

get squeezed by a giant Pacific octopus *or* get slimed by a vampire squid?"

"Shh!" said Stink.

"Then one night—they say it happened during a sleepover—"

"Like this one?" asked Webster.

"On a night not unlike tonight, Bloody Mary stretched out her long filaments to grab some yummy fish eyes and zap! *ZZZZZ!* She stuck a filament into an electrical outlet outside the tank, and she was changed forever."

"What happened?" Sophie asked.

"Frankensquid! She grew two heads,

multiple arms, and opened only one eye. True to her vampire nature, she began thirsting for the blood of the living and the undead."

"No way is that true, right?" asked Stink.

Miss D. shrugged. Her eyes glowed in the dim light. "Who's to say?"

"Then what happened?"

"Searching for blood, she slithered out of her tank and across the slippery floor of Sharks Ahoy, where a group of kids were sleeping. Just as the kids were about to get slimed, they woke up and shooed her into a dark room, slammed the door, and locked it, trapping her inside. No one has seen her since she disappeared behind that very door."

"That's why it says keep out?" asked Stink. Miss D. nodded.

"*D* is for *Don't Go Behind That Door*," said Sophie, shivering.

"So if you see a red glow coming from under a door, do not open it: Bloody Mary is on the prowl and strange things can happen."

"Like what?"

"A chill wind blows, but no window is

open. A phone rings, but nobody is there. Some say that on sleepover nights, you might hear the ghost of Bloody Mary the vampire squid moaning and groaning."

Stink shivered. Webster wiggled his wobbly tooth.

"If you look into her eyes, she'll turn you to blood and drink you up."

The kids fell silent.

"Unless . . ." Miss D. went on.

"Unless what?" asked Stink and Webster at the same time.

"Unless you can say *Bloody Mary* three times fast!"

"Bloody Mary, Bloody Mary, Bloody Mary," the kids said super fast.

"And that is the story of Bloody Mary," said Miss D. "Now, who wants waffles?"

"Bloody Mary, Bloody Mary, Bloody Mary," Stink whispered one last time, just to be on the safe side.

VAMPIRE SQUID

It's an octopus! No, it's a squid! No, it's a vampire!

The vampire squid is related to the squid and octopus. Its black or bloodred color and spooky eyes give it its name. A web like a vampire's cloak connects its eight arms.

Nom, Nom, Nom.

Vampire squids eat "marine snow"— dead sea creatures, poop, and snot. No lie!

When in danger, a vampire squid turns itself inside-out, showing off wicked-looking spines that scare away attackers.

Squids squirt ink to confuse their predators. Vampire squids shoot out glow-in-the-dark slime instead. These orbs of blue light daze the attacker. Poof! The squid gets away.

Webster took one last bite of his waffle. Sophie mopped up the last of her maple syrup.

"How can you guys even *think* about waffles at a time like this?" Stink asked.

"A time like what?" Webster asked.

"Hel-lo! Bloody Mary? I'll never be able to sleep now. Not in a million years." Stink scooched closer to Sophie and Webster.

Just then, Miss D. made an announcement. "It's been a great night, everybody. But this is a *sleep*over. Time to join your group or family. Let's all get some shut-eye."

Stink shivered at the thought of trying to sleep, in the dark, with sharks. Not to mention Bloody You-Know-Who.

"One of our staff will be on call all night," said Miss D. "If you need anything, talk to the person at the info desk."

"C'mon, Mr. Crab Cakes. Time for bed," Sophie said, then yawned. "Stink, where is your family set up?"

"Not far enough away from that

door," Stink said. "Go up the ramp, turn left, and they're at the other end of Sharks Ahoy."

Suddenly, the aquarium felt a lot darker. Gurgling and burbling sounds coming from the tanks seemed a lot creepier.

Clumps of families and kids in sleeping bags were already asleep on the floor of Sharks Ahoy. Mom, Dad, and Judy were playing a game of Go Fish.

"Did you have fun?" asked Dad.

"Yeah, until Bloody Mary," said Stink.

"Bloody who?" asked Judy. Stink

pointed to the KEEP OUT door at the other end of Sharks Ahoy. He told Judy all about the vampire squid.

"Creep-a-zoidal," said Judy.

Everybody snuggled down into sleeping bags. Mom and Dad were softly snoring in no time.

Even Mr. Crab Cakes was tucked away in his coconut-shell hut. "Night, Mr. Crab Cakes," said Sophie. "See you in the morning."

"I have an idea," said Stink. "Let's all three of us promise not to fall asleep tonight. We can shake on it with our new handshake."

"New handshake?" asked Sophie.

"Hold out your arm, like this." Stink held out his arm, wiggled his fingers on top of Sophie's, then slowly pulled it back.

"That tickles," said Sophie.

"It's the vampire-squid handshake," said Stink.

"Can't," said Sophie, rubbing her eyes. "I'm too tired."

"Me, too," said Webster, yawning.

Sophie fell asleep as soon as her head hit the pillow. Webster took off his glasses and hunkered down in the bag next to Stink's.

"Webster?" Stink whispered. But his friend was already fast asleep.

The bluey-green light from the shark tanks cast a ghostly glow over the room. A pointy-nosed tiger shark streaked by, eyeing Stink and showing off his jagged teeth. A smack of goose bumps—a swarm, a fleet, a bloom of goose bumps—prickled up and down Stink's spine. *What if the shark tank broke and all the sharks got out?*

He missed his own room. With his very own race-car bed and Astro and Toady and his Spider-Man, not-baby night-light.

He squeezed his eyes shut. He tried counting shark teeth. He tried counting moon jellies in the ocean. *What if Bloody Mary reached out and slimed me?*

"Judy?" He crawled over and gave his sister a nudge. "You asleep?"

"Yes, I'm asleep," Judy mumbled.

"I can't sleep," said Stink.

"Try counting shark teeth."

"Tried. But now I'm afraid I'll have shark-eating-me dreams."

"So count pancakes. Silver-dollar pancakes aren't scary."

Stink counted silver-dollar pancakes. "Now I'm hungry," whispered Stink.

"Judy? Are you asleep over there?"

No answer.

Stink leaned over and gave Webster a nudge. "Hey. Webster. Let's play a prank on Judy."

Webster rubbed his eyes and sat up. "Prank. What kind of prank?"

"A sleepover prank!" said Stink, feeling better already. "We could . . . tie her feet together while she's sleeping."

"Do you have any string? Or rope?"

"Nope on the rope," said Stink.

"We could stick her hand in a cup of water," said Webster.

"What for?" asked Stink.

"To make her wet the bed!"

"Yeah!" said Stink. "Do you have a cup of water?"

Webster looked in his snack pack. "I have an empty juice box, some ketchup packets, and four baloney-sandwich bread crusts."

"Hey, I know." Stink poked around in his backpack and then held up a marker. "Let's draw a mustache on her."

They crawled over to Judy. Webster held a flashlight while Stink held out his marker. Judy stirred. "Hey! What are you doing?"

"Nothing," said Stink.

"You better not be trying to mus-tache me," said Judy.

"Rats," said Stink. Judy pulled the sleeping bag over her head.

"Do you have any deodorant?" whispered Webster.

Stink crawled over and got deodor-ant from Dad's shaving kit.

"Okay," said Webster. "Put the deodorant under her nose . . ."

"Uh-huh?"

"And when she smells it . . ."

"Uh-huh?"

"It will make her sleep talk."

"Sleep walk?"

"No, sleep talk. Talk in her sleep."

Stink crawled back over to Judy. He pulled back the top of the sleeping bag. He took the cap off of the deodorant, and passed it right under her nose.

Judy swiped at her nose. She sneezed. Her lips moved.

"It's working!" whispered Stink.

Judy mumbled four words.

"What did she say?" asked Webster.

"She said, 'I heart Frank Pearl.' My sister's in love with Frank Pearl!"

"That's not what she said. She said 'I fart prank girl.'"

"That doesn't even make sense!" said Stink. They cracked up so bad it woke Sophie of the Elves.

"What's so funny?" she asked.

"Your hair is sticking up like a sea urchin!" said Webster.

Sophie mashed her sticky-up hair down. "So what?" She aimed her flashlight at the hermit-crab habitat. She put on her glasses and peered closer. "Mr. Crab Cakes?"

"What's wrong?" asked Stink.

"Mr. Crab Cakes! He's not here! As in G-O-N-E *gone*!" She picked up the habitat and held it out for them to see.

"Are you sure?"

"Sure I'm sure. He was right here in his little hut when I went to sleep. But he's not hiding under the bridge or in his crab shack or anywhere. We have to find him!"

"Search party!" said Stink.

The three friends, flashlights in hands, looked in their sleeping bags. *Under* their sleeping bags. Stink looked all around Judy and Mom and Dad. Webster even looked in Sophie's sea-urchin hair. Sophie turned her pj pockets inside out.

No Mr. Crab Cakes.

"Hey, look!" said Sophie, pointing to a trail of water drips and drops. "I think Mr. Crab Cakes left a trail."

On hands and knees, they followed the trail until they came to a door.

But it was not just any door. It was *the* door. The KEEP OUT door.

"Bloody Mary!" said Stink.

BLOODY MARY

GET YOUR SCARE ON!

"Bloody Mary" is a popular scary story told at sleepovers. In some versions, she's called Mary Worth or Mary White. She is usually a witch or a ghost. But at an aquarium, why not a vampire squid?

Legend has it that if you stand in front of a mirror and say "Bloody Mary" three times fast, she will appear!

If she does, look out! Bloody Mary likes to scream, scratch, and drink blood, and she might try to pull you into the mirror.

Whoooo!

I'm not going back there," Stink said.

"Well, don't look at me," said Webster. "Besides, it says KEEP OUT. Mr. Crab Cakes wouldn't go in there."

"Hermit crabs can't read," said Sophie.

"Judy. Let's get Judy!" said Stink. They hurried back to the far end of Sharks Ahoy. Judy was sound asleep.

"Webster. Get a ketchup packet. Stat," said Stink.

Stink squirted ketchup all over his hand. He held his ketchup-y hand in front of her face. He whisper-yelled into her ear, "Shark attack! Shark attack! Aagh! My hand!"

Judy bolted awake. "Stink. Your hand! What happened—?"

Stink licked the ketchup off his hand. "Pranked you. We got you so good."

"ROAR!" Judy growled.

"Now that you're awake," said Stink, "we need your help."

"Mr. Crab Cakes is lost," said Sophie. "Our search party followed a trail of water drips. We think he crawled under the KEEP OUT door."

"We're afraid Bloody Mary might have gotten him," said Webster.

Judy rubbed her eyes. "If I help, you have to promise to let me go back to sleep. And not play any more pranks on me tonight?"

Stink held out his shark-tooth neck-lace. "I shark-swear it."

Judy Moody led the way to the KEEP OUT door. The low moo of a whale groaned in the background. She reached for the door handle.

"Wait!" whispered Stink. "First make sure there's no spooky red glow com-ing from under the door."

Judy bent down to look. "No red glow, Stink." She put her ear to the door. "Shh. I hear something."

"Is it a phone ringing?" asked Webster.

"It's not a phone ringing," said Judy.

"Is it a moaning? Or a groaning?" asked Sophie.

"More like a humming," said Judy.

Stink gulped. Webster went as pale as a moon jelly. Sophie covered up her ears. "Bloody Mary!" they all screeched, huddling together like a waddle of penguins.

But Judy was already turning the handle. A strange sound echoed suddenly in the dark. *Aii ooh eee moo . . .*

Before you could say one-two-three-squidoo, Stink and his friends jumped back, hanging on to one another.

"Let's look for Mr. Crab Cakes tomorrow," said Sophie. Stink nodded.

"No way am I going in there," said Webster.

"Psych!" Judy grinned. "Gotcha back, Stink. That was just me."

"You spooked the goose bumps right off of me!" said Stink.

"C'mon." Judy opened the KEEP OUT

door, shining her flashlight left and right. Trays of bones! Boxes of claws! Jars of eyeballs! "This looks like a work-room," said Judy.

✴ ✴ ✴

They followed the beam of light, searching under table after table for Sophie's hermit crab.

"He could be anywhere," said Sophie.

"I hope a tiger shark didn't eat him," said Stink.

"Or a bat ray," said Webster. "Or a giant octopus."

Stink shook off a shiver. "Maybe they're putting skeletons together here.

Maybe it's a bazillion-million-year-old *Megaxantho* skeleton."

"What's a *Megaxantho*?" asked Sophie.

"Giant prehistoric crab," said Stink.

"Hey, maybe it's the great-great-great-great-grandfather of Mr. Crab Cakes," said Sophie.

Suddenly, in the beam of flashlight, a giant pincher appeared. It seemed to reach out—

"Attack of the Japanese giant spider crab!" cried Stink. He tripped over his own foot, knocking into Sophie. Sophie fell back and knocked into Webster. Her elbow hit him square in the mouth.

"Tooth! My tooth!" Judy aimed her flashlight at Webster. He showed off the hole where his tooth had been.

"My loose tooth!" he said, holding up a pointy little tooth. "Hey, I can talk again."

"I bet it's at least one-sixteenth shark tooth," said Stink.

"You can put it under your pillow tonight," said Sophie.

"Does the Tooth Fairy stay up this late?" asked Webster.

"Sure," said Sophie.

Just then, they heard a sound. A purring sound. *For real.* Judy tilted an ear to listen. "It's coming from over there. Behind that door."

They tiptoed across the lab to another door. Sophie held her breath.

Stink pointed to the bottom of the door. A ghostly red glow spilled out from the crack under the door. It made their faces look Halloween-spooky.

Purrrrrrrrr.

"Judy! Did you hear that? Don't go in there," warned Stink.

"There could be a killer shark in there," said Webster. "I think I hear him grinding his teeth."

"Bloody Mary!" said Sophie, holding on to Stink's sleeve.

The three friends hung back as Judy opened the door. She took one step into the reddish darkness. She felt for a light switch.

The beast purred again, louder. Stink shivered. "Does anybody else feel a cold breeze?"

Just then, the light came on. Stink
and Sophie and Webster could not
believe their eyes.

A kitchen!

They were in a kitchen. A fridge
purred. A microwave blinked.

"It's the lunchroom," said Judy.

The fridge made a loud gurgly
sound. "Here's your vampire squid,"
said Judy, pointing to the ice-maker.
She opened the freezer and a blast of
cold air came out in a misty puff. "And
here's your cold breeze."

"But how could—" said Stink.

"Meet Bloody Mary," said Judy. She

pointed to the clock with glowing red numbers on the microwave oven.

"Bloody Mary is Bloody *Microwave*?" asked Stink. Judy nodded.

"Phew," said Sophie and Webster, plopping down in some chairs.

"Hey! We could make popcorn!"

"Stink. Are you nuts? Do you know what would happen if we got caught?"

"No, what?" Stink whispered.

"They'd let the vampire squid suck out all your blood," said Judy.

Just then, the phone rang. Stink reached to pick it up. "Don't—" said Judy. But it was too late.

"Hello?" asked Stink.

There was no answer.

"Hello?" Stink asked again.

Still no answer.

"Nobody's there." Stink looked at Sophie. Sophie looked at Webster.

"Bloody Mary, Bloody Mary, Bloody

Mary!" all three shouted, racing out the door, down the hall, past Mr. Crab Cakes's great-great-great-great-grandfather, past *Megaxantho*, past trays of bones and boxes of claws, out through the KEEP OUT door, and back into the bluey-green night-light glow of Sharks Ahoy.

They were all out of breath by the time they got back to their sleeping bags. Stink's heart was still drum-beating in his chest.

Judy came up behind them and crawled into her bag. Sophie pulled her bag up to her chin.

"Sorry we didn't find Mr. Crab Cakes," Stink said to Sophie.

"We'll search again in the morning. In the light." Sophie let out a yawn.

"Good night, sleep tight," said Stink. "Don't let the jellyfish bite!"

He tried to quiet his thumping heart, but Stink couldn't stop thinking about Bloody Mary. "Hey, Webster. Let's go brush our teeth one more time."

✳ ✳ ✳

Webster looked in the restroom mirror. He stuck his finger in the hole where his tooth had been.

"Does it hurt?" Stink asked.

"Nah. It just feels funny. But it makes me look so cool! Like a bad-guy pirate."

Stink squeezed the toothpaste too fast and it got on his finger. Then he scratched his nose.

"You have green gunk on your nose," said Webster. "And it's *snot* snot!"

"Hey, now I know how I can prank Judy. For realsies. C'mon. Bring toothpaste."

"But she said no more pranks. And you promised."

"She said no more pranks *tonight*. But it's one minute after midnight! So that was *last* night. Besides, I had my fingers crossed."

Judy was dead to the world. Stink squirted toothpaste on the tips of her fingers. Then he blew on her face.

Judy reached up to scratch her nose. She scratched her forehead. In no time, she had ooey-gooey green toothpaste all over her face!

"Judy is going to think she got vampire-squid slimed!" said Stink, pleased with himself.

Finally, Stink and Webster crawled inside their sleeping bags. Even Stink was dog tired now. Dog*fish* tired.

Webster put his tooth in the blue-shark Tooth-Fairy pillow. He put the blue-shark Tooth-Fairy pillow under his regular pillow.

"Night, Sting," he whispered.

But all the Sting had already gone out of Stink. He did not have to count sharks or pancakes or sheep. He was *Z-for-Zonked-Out.*

* * *

The next morning, Stink woke up to see sharks zooming around their tanks. He rolled over. "Webster? You awake?"

"Huh? Wha?" Webster felt for his glasses and put them on. "Oh, it's you. I thought you were the Tooth Fairy."

He reached under his pillow and pulled out his Tooth-Fairy pillow. He felt inside the shark's mouth. "My tooth is still in here. And there's no money!"

Webster showed Sophie. "Nada. Big fat zero."

"Don't worry," said Sophie, who was already awake. "The Tooth Fairy just didn't know you were on a sleepover at the aquarium."

"Really?" said Webster.

"Trust me. I'm an expert when it comes to all things Toot Fairy."

"Toot Fairy?" Webster cracked up.

"That's what my little sister, Mimi, calls the Tooth Fairy."

Just then, Judy sat up. Her hair was a bird's-nest mess. Her face was a map of green polka dots.

"Measles! You have green measles!" Sophie cried. "On your face!"

Stink and Webster laughed their pajama pants off.

"What?" Judy asked. She touched her face. Not one, not two, but three green measles fell into her hand.

Judy jumped up and ran for the bathroom. "I'm going to get you for this, Stinker!"

Mom and Dad came over, sipping cups of steaming coffee. "How did everybody sleep?" Dad asked.

"I slept *all night* with the sharks and I wasn't even scared," said Stink.

"Good for you," said Mom, rubbing her neck.

Dad rubbed his back. "It must be twenty-five years since I've been on a sleepover," he said, wincing.

"And I bet you were never on a *shark* sleepover," said Stink.

"It's a first," Dad agreed.

Judy came back dressed in clothes-not-pajamas, with her face newly washed and scrubbed. "I still feel toothpaste measles on my cheeks. I'm gonna get you, Stinkerbell. And, like a slippery silent shark, you'll never see me coming."

Judy bent down to put on her shoes. "Aagh!" she yelled, kicking one off and hopping on one foot. "You are toast, Stink Moody. Dead meat."

"What did I do?" Stink asked.

"You put something pinchy in my shoe, didn't you?" Judy peered inside her shoe. "Hey!" she said, then reached in and pulled out . . .

"Mr. Crab Cakes!" Sophie yelled. "You found my hermit crab!" Sophie scooped the crab up in her hand and hugged him to her. "I thought you were gone forever, Mr. Crab Cakes." She kissed him on the shell.

"This wasn't a prank? All this time, Mr. Crab Cakes was hiding in my shoe for real?" Judy asked.

"I so did not hermit-crab you. Shark's honor!" said Stink.

"All's well that ends well," said Dad.

"Let's eat some breakfast before we leave," said Mom. "I hear they make a killer shark fruit salad."

"And jellyfish muffins," said Dad.

✳ ✳ ✳

"Team Sharkfinder," said Miss D. at breakfast, "what were your favorite things at the aquarium?"

"The bloodybelly comb jelly!" said Webster.

"I have three favorite things," said Sophie of the Elves. "Goblin shark, fairy penguin, and Medusa jellyfish."

"She likes all things fairies, elves, and goblins," Webster explained.

"Megalodon shark fin," said Stink.

"Miss D.," said Sophie, "we never did guess your name. *D* is for *Dogfish*?"

"Nope."

"*D* is for *Doughnut*?" asked Webster.

"Nope."

"*D* is for *Doorstop*?" asked Stink.

Miss D. laughed. "I hope not."

"We give up," said Sophie.

"My real name is Danielle . . ."

"Danielle what?"

"Danielle Dangermaus."

"Danger Mouse?" asked Sophie. "That's like the coolest name *ever!*"

"Like the cartoon?" said Webster. "He's that mouse with an eye patch who gets attacked by robots and washing machines and vampire ducks."

"I knew it. You're like a secret agent spy or something," said Sophie.

"Can I make a comic book of you?" asked Stink. "You could be a superhero mouse that fights crime with a supersonic jelly-fish sting."

"I'd be honored," said Miss D.

Mom and Dad came over to say good-bye to Miss D., too. "This was such a great experience for the kids," said Mom. "Thanks so much."

Dad smiled at Stink. "Much better than any old doorstop."

"Or a cookbook," said Mom, winking.

Dad shook Miss D.'s hand. "You just shook hands with Danger Mouse," said Stink. "Secret agent super-spy."

"Guys! Check it out!" Judy said, running over to them. "I got a fish-eye camera at the gift shop. It takes real pictures, but they come out looking like you're in a goldfish bowl."

"How'd you get the money?"

Judy ignored the question. "Don't you want to see what you'd look like from inside a goldfish bowl?"

"Yeah!" said Stink. "Let's wear our T-shirts and take pictures with Sharkzilla."

They all gathered in front of the seven-foot shark fin. "Don't forget me!" said Rotten Riley, jumping into the picture.

Judy pointed the camera at them. "Say *Sharkzilla!*"

"Sharkzilla!" they all said, smiling ear to ear.

"Hey, Stink," said Riley. "Would you rather move in next door to Bloody Mary or live inside a giant clam?"

"Giant clam any day," said Stink.

"Okay. Here's one. Would you rather have a giant Pacific octopus for a pet *or* have a seven-foot dorsal fin from Sharkzilla planted in your front yard?"

"Sharkzilla fin," said Stink. "No, wait. Giant octopus. No, wait. Sharkzilla."

"Bye, everybody," said Riley. "See you at school on Monday!" They all wiggled their fingers and slipped one another the vampire-squid handshake.

"Wait just a shark-fin minute!" said Stink. He waved his Stinger Finger in the air. "I got one. Would you rather ride on the back of a killer whale *or* go on a shark sleepover?"

"Shark sleepover!" everybody yelled.

Megan McDonald ————————

is the author of the popular Judy Moody and Stink series. She says, "Once, while I was visiting a class, the kids chanted, 'Stink! Stink! Stink!' as I entered the room. In that moment, I knew that Stink had to have a series all his own." Megan McDonald lives in California.

Peter H. Reynolds ————————

is the illustrator of all the Judy Moody and Stink books. He says, "Stink reminds me of myself growing up: dealing with a sister prone to teasing and bossing around—and having to get creative in order to stand tall beside her." Peter H. Reynolds lives in Massachusetts.

BE SURE TO CHECK OUT ALL OF STINK'S ADVENTURES!

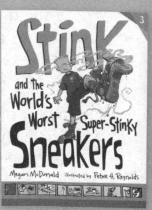

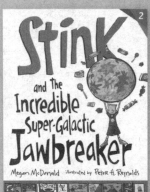

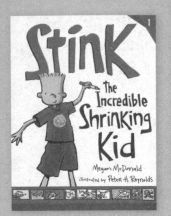

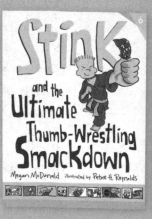

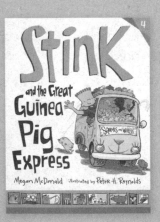

STINK HAS HIS OWN SUPER WEBSITE!

www.stinkmoody.com

Grab even more Stink with these paperback collections!

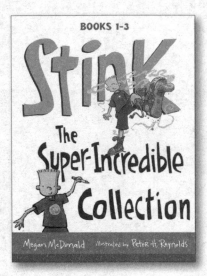

Rumple-STINK-skin! Make sure you don't miss a single smelly story with Stink's first three way-cool adventures.

What do 101 guinea pigs, the Planet Test, and an imperfect report card have in common? They're all in this boxed set of Stink's fourth, fifth, and sixth adventures!

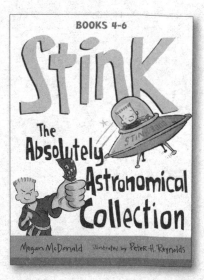

Judy Moody and Stink
are starring together!

In full color!

Need more Moody?

Try These!

Stink

has his own super website!

www.stinkmoody.com

Go online to:

- Make your own comics.

- Host your own Way-Official Moody Stink-a-thon.

- Help Astro with a guinea pig maze.

- Read exclusive excerpts from Stink's books.

- Find lots of Stink-y information and activities!